KU-339-601

This book belongs to

_____

_____

This edition published by Parragon Books Ltd in 2015

Parragon Books Ltd
Chartist House
15–17 Trim Street
Bath BA1 1HA, UK
www.parragon.com

Copyright © 2015 Disney Enterprises, Inc.

All rights reserved. No part of this publication may be reproduced, stored in a retrieval
system or transmitted, in any form or by any means, electronic, mechanical, photocopying,
recording or otherwise, without the prior permission of the copyright holder.

ISBN 978-1-4723-8200-9

Printed in China

DISNEY MOVIE COLLECTION
A SPECIAL DISNEY STORYBOOK SERIES

Peter Pan

PaRRagon
Bath · New York · Cologne · Melbourne · Delhi
Hong Kong · Shenzhen · Singapore · Amsterdam

There was once a house in London where Mr and Mrs Darling and their three children, Wendy, John and Michael, lived. Watching over the children was Nana, the nursemaid, who also happened to be a dog. It was to this home that Peter Pan came one magical night.

He chose this house for one very special reason: there were people there who believed in him. But not Mr Darling – he only thought about business, the importance of being on time and dressing properly.

But Mrs Darling was still young enough at heart to believe in Peter Pan and that he was the spirit of youth.

Then there were John and Michael.
They knew how to fight off pirates,
whoop like Indians and march like soldiers.
To them Peter Pan was certainly real and
they made him the hero of all their games.

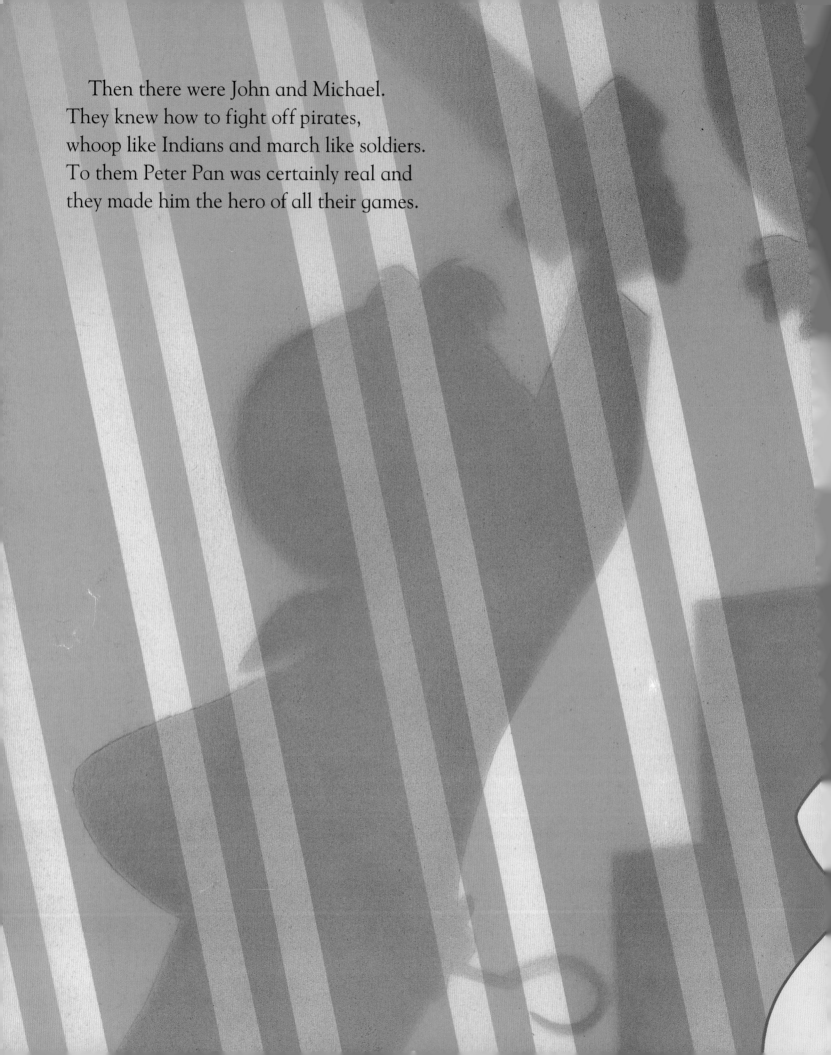

But the real expert on Peter Pan was Wendy. She knew everything there was to know about him.

On this particular night, after Michael and John had drawn a pirate map on their father's shirt, Mr Darling angrily declared, "Children need to grow up." Then, turning to Wendy, he added, "This is your last night in the nursery, young lady."

Mrs Darling tucked her three children into bed and kissed them goodnight. Then she and Mr Darling left for a party, leaving Wendy, John and Michael fast asleep.

As soon as the children were asleep, Peter Pan and his fairy friend, Tinker Bell,
slipped in through the window. The Darlings' nursery was a familiar place to Peter.
He liked to sit in the shadows and listen to Wendy's stories about Never Land.
But on his last visit, Peter had been separated from his shadow.
Tonight he had come to get it back.

"Well done, Tink, you've found it!" Peter whispered
when Tinker Bell discovered his shadow.

But the shadow was in no hurry to be caught,
it flitted and skittered around the room.
Peter charged after it, making such a racket
that Wendy woke up.

"Peter Pan! I knew you'd come!"
Wendy cried. "I saved your shadow for
you. Let me sew it back on. Oh, Peter,
I'm so glad you came back tonight
because it's my last night in the nursery,"
she added sadly.

"But that means no more stories!"
cried Peter. "I won't have it! Come on,
we're going to Never Land. You'll never
grow up there!"

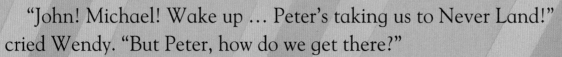

"John! Michael! Wake up … Peter's taking us to Never Land!"
cried Wendy. "But Peter, how do we get there?"

"Fly, of course. It's easy. All you have to do is think a wonderful thought.
And … " said Peter, shaking Tinker Bell, " … add a little bit of pixie dust."

"We can fly!" announced Wendy,
John and Michael as they followed
Peter and Tink out of the nursery
window. They soared over the rooftops
of London.

Peter laughed with glee as he pointed
up into the sky.

"There it is, Wendy – Never Land.
Second star to the right and straight
on 'til morning."

From high up in the sky, they finally spotted the land of their dreams.
"Look, John," cried Wendy, "Mermaid Lagoon!"
"And the Indian Camp!" yelled John.
"There's the pirate ship and its crew," added Michael. "It's just as you told us, Wendy!"

The captain of the pirate ship was Hook. He hated Peter Pan.

"Blast that Peter Pan!" Hook said to his first mate, Mr Smee, as he studied a map of Never Land. "If I could only find his hideout, I'd trap him."

Captain Hook got his name because he had a hook where his hand should have been. And who was to blame for that? Why, Peter Pan, of course!

Hook had another enemy, too – the crocodile.

"He's been following me around for years, licking his chops," said Hook.

"And he'd have had you by now, Cap'n, if he hadn't swallowed that alarm clock. Now when he's about, he warns you with his tick-tock, tick-tock...." said Smee.

"Peter Pan, ahoy!" cried the lookout.

Captain Hook forgot about the crocodile instantly.
"Blast!" he cried, looking through his telescope. "It is
Pan!" He ordered his men to load the cannon and fire!

"Quick, Tink!" shouted Peter as the cannonballs
flew by. "Take Wendy and the boys to the island!
I'll stay here and cause a diversion!"

Tinker Bell took off at once and flew straight to Peter's
hideout. But she purposely flew too fast, leaving the others
far behind.

"Tinker Bell! Wait for us! We can't keep up with you!"
yelled Wendy and the boys.

But Tink didn't want to wait. Peter Pan
had hardly looked at Tinker Bell since
Wendy had come along. Tink didn't like
it one bit and now she had a plan.

Tinker Bell zoomed ahead, flying through an opening in a tree to where the Lost Boys and Peter lived.

She told the boys Peter had sent her with a message that there was a terrible 'Wendy-bird' headed their way. Peter's orders were to shoot it down.

The Lost Boys hurried out from their hiding place.

"I see it!" yelled Skunk as he and the others placed stones in their catapults.

"Ready … aim … fire!" shouted the boys. Suddenly rocks were flying everywhere, hitting Wendy and sending her tumbling from the sky!

Luckily, Peter Pan arrived just in time to catch Wendy.

"Peter … you saved my life," said Wendy, throwing her arms around him.

"I bring you a mother to tell you stories," Peter angrily told the Lost Boys, "and you shoot her down!"

"B-b-but Tink said it was a bird," stammered Cubby.

"She said you wanted us to shoot it," added Rabbit.

"Tinker Bell," said Peter, "you might have killed Wendy! I hereby banish you forever!"

"Please," begged Wendy, feeling sorry for poor Tinker Bell, "not forever!"

"For a week, then," declared Peter.

Taking Wendy by the hand, Peter flew off to show her
Mermaid Lagoon. John and Michael wanted to explore
Never Land too, but had no interest in mermaids.
They wanted to see Indians.

"John, you be the leader," declared the Lost Boys.
Then, lining up behind him, they all marched off into
the forest.

As they marched along, the Lost Boys and John
made a plan. They would be very clever and capture
the Indians!

It might have worked, except for one thing – the Indians caught them first.

Michael and John were very frightened until the Lost Boys explained how things worked. "When we win, we let them go. When they win, they let us go."

But this time the Indian Chief wouldn't set the Lost Boys free. He thought they had kidnapped his daughter, Tiger Lily.

"You tell me where you hid the Princess Tiger Lily," the chief said, "or you'll be punished!"

Meanwhile, Peter was showing Wendy the beautiful Mermaid Lagoon. Wendy thought the mermaids were lovely. The mermaids couldn't say the same about Wendy. They thought she looked silly in her nightgown. And they didn't like that she was friends with Peter!

While Wendy was fending off the jealous mermaids, Peter had spotted Hook and Smee rowing by in a small boat. Tied up in the back was Tiger Lily!

Peter and Wendy flew off for Skull Rock to see what Hook and Smee were up to. From a cliff, they peered down at Captain Hook and his prisoner.

Captain Hook was threatening Tiger Lily. "If you don't tell me where Pan's hiding place is, I'll leave you here on the rock for when the tide comes in!"

But Tiger Lily just held her head up proudly and refused to give Peter away.

"I'll show the old codfish," said Peter. "Stay here, Wendy, and watch the fun!"

Peter shouted: "Captain Hook, you're a codfish!"

Hook and Smee looked up in amazement. Hook drew his sword and leapt up to attack Peter. He lunged at him, but Peter was too nimble. He drove the Captain crazy, prancing and dancing around him and dodging every thrust of the sword. Then Peter pinned the captain, but Hook broke free and fought Peter to the very edge of a cliff.

"I've got you this time, Pan!" he cried. Peter backed away from Hook.

Hook followed. "Aaaahhhh!" he screamed, as he tumbled off the cliff and into the lagoon. "I'll get you for this, Pan!" he yelled. As he fell towards the water, Hook heard a familiar sound … tick-tock, tick-tock, tick-tock.

"I say, Hook," said Peter Pan, "do you hear something?"

The captain desperately kicked his feet away from the crocodile's sharp teeth, screaming: "Smee! Save me! Smeeeeeee!"

Peter was laughing his head off when Wendy reminded him about Tiger Lily. The brave Indian Princess already had water right up to her chin! Peter swooped down to save Tiger Lily and flew her back home.

The Indian Chief was so happy to see his daughter again that he freed John, Michael and the Lost Boys. Then he placed a headdress of beautiful feathers on Peter Pan, proclaiming him to be 'Chief Little Flying Eagle'.

"Waaawhoop!" yelled Peter.

"Oh, how wonderful!" said Wendy.

"Bravo!" added John.

But there was someone who was not joining in the celebration.
Poor Tinker Bell was sat all alone without Peter or her friends,
the Lost Boys. And she wasn't happy at all.
    And that's just how Mr Smee found Tinker Bell … all alone,
sitting by herself.

"Beggin' your pardon, Miss Bell,"
said Smee, catching Tinker Bell in
his hat, "but Cap'n Hook would like
a word with you if you don't mind."

Aboard the pirate ship, Captain Hook was telling Tinker Bell his plan.

"We sail in the morning," he told Tinker Bell. If she would only tell him where Peter's hideout was, he promised to take Wendy off to sea with him.

"With her gone, Peter will soon forget this mad infatuation!" sneered the captain.

Sick with jealousy and loneliness, Tinker Bell fell for Hook's evil plan and showed him how to find Peter's hideaway.

Hook smiled, then he grabbed Tinker Bell and locked her in a glass lantern. At last he could get his revenge on Peter Pan once and for all!

At Peter's hideaway, all was cosy and quiet. Wendy, acting as a good mother should, was tucking the boys into bed. As she did, she sang to them about the wonders of a real mother. By the time Wendy had finished her song, John and Michael were so homesick that they wanted to leave for London immediately. Even the Lost Boys wanted to go.

But not Peter. "Go back and grow up? No!" he said stubbornly. "I'm warning you, once you're grown up, you can never come back!"

But no one was listening to Peter. They had only one thought on their minds: a mother to love them and hold them and sing them to sleep at night.

One by one, Wendy and the boys left Peter's hideaway – only to walk right into a trap and the arms of the waiting pirates!

Before returning to his ship with the prisoners, Hook lowered a beautifully wrapped package into Peter Pan's hideout.

Tying his prisoners to the mast of the ship, Hook warned them, "Join us or walk the plank."

"Never," declared Wendy. "Peter Pan will save us."

"My dear," said Hook, "we left a present for Peter, a sort of surprise. I can see our little friend at this very moment, reading the tender note: 'To Peter, with love, from Wendy.' But if he could see within the package, he would find a little device set so that when it is six o'clock, he will be blasted out of Never Land forever!"

After hearing Hook's evil plan, Tinker Bell escaped and rushed to Peter Pan's hideout.

Peter was just untying the bow on the package when Tinker Bell flew in.

"Hi, Tink," said Peter, holding up the box. "Look what Wendy left."

Tinker Bell tried to pull the package away. "Stop that!" yelled Peter. "What's the matter with you?"

There was no time to explain. Tink flew at the box, pushing it as far from Peter as she could. The gift began to smoke and then … KABOOM!

The explosion was so huge, it rocked the pirate ship out at sea! Hook removed his hat and bowed. "And so passeth a worthy opponent!"

Thinking t
to the captiv
the plank?"
    Wendy s
ever join yc
    Hook g
my dear!"
the plank
    One st
finally, sh
    "Cap'
    "The
But it

As Wendy, John, Michael and the Lost Boys fought the pirate crew, Peter and Hook continued to battle, until Hook disarmed him!

Peter jumped up, grabbed a pirate flag and wrapped it around Hook. The fight was over – Peter had won! But when Peter turned his back, Hook freed himself and lunged with his sword. Peter jumped out of the way, causing Hook to lose his balance! Down he fell to face his worst fear – the crocodile was waiting and its mouth was wide open!

Hook emerged between the crocodile's jaws, screaming for Smee to come and rescue him. Smee and the other pirates had all taken refuge in a row boat and were rowing away as fast as they could. Captain Hook leapt out of the crocodile's jaws and started swimming after his crew, with the crocodile close behind him!

"Hooray for Captain Pan!" screamed the children.

"All right, ya swabs," said Peter Pan to his brand-new crew, "we're castin' off! Set sail for London!"

Wendy smiled.

"Hoist the anchor!" cried Peter. "Tink, let's have some pixie dust!"

Tinker Bell flew all around the ship, sprinkling her magical dust as she went. Then, up, up, up went the ship and, as it rose, it began to glow like gold. Wendy was sad to be leaving Never Land, but she was excited to be going home.

"Wendy," said Mrs Darling. She was gently shaking her daughter, whom she had found asleep by the window.

"Oh, Mother, we're back!" announced Wendy as she woke.

"Back?" asked Mr Darling.

"All except the Lost Boys," explained Wendy. "They weren't quite ready to grow up. It was such an adventure! Tinker Bell and mermaids and Peter Pan. We sailed away in a ship in the sky...."

"Mary," said Mr Darling, not sharing Wendy's excitement at all, "I'm going to bed."

But as he turned to leave, Mr Darling paused to look up into the night sky. There, crossing in front of the moon, was a ship made of clouds.

"You know," said Mr Darling, "I have the strangest feeling I've seen that ship before. A long time ago, when I was very young."

And, indeed, he had.